What's on the Menu?

Food Poems selected by

BOBBYE S. GOLDSTEIN

Illustrated by

CHRIS L. DEMAREST

Viking

For my sisters,
Eleanor and Shirley,
with love
—B.S.G.

For Jill and Rob,
my favorite chefs
—C.L.D.

VIKING
Published by the Penguin Group
Viking Penguin, a division of Penguin Books USA Inc.,
375 Hudson Street, New York, New York 10014, U.S.A.
Penguin Books Ltd, 27 Wrights Lane, London W8 5TZ, England
Penguin Books Australia Ltd, Ringwood, Victoria, Australia
Penguin Books Canada Ltd, 10 Alcorn Avenue, Toronto, Ontario, Canada M4V 3B2
Penguin Books (N.Z.) Ltd, 182–190 Wairau Road, Auckland 10, New Zealand
Penguin Books Ltd, Registered Offices: Harmondsworth, Middlesex, England
First published in 1992 by Viking Penguin, a division of Penguin Books USA Inc.

1   3   5   7   9   10   8   6   4   2

Text copyright © Bobbye S. Goldstein, 1992
Illustrations copyright © Chris L. Demarest, 1992
All rights reserved
Page 32 constitutes an extension of this copyright page.

Library of Congress Cataloging-in-Publication Data
What's on the menu? / selected by Bobbye S. Goldstein ;
illustrated by Chris L. Demarest   p.   cm.
Summary: A collection of poems about the tasty world of food,
from lumpy bumpy pickles to chunky chocolate cake.
ISBN 0-670-83031-3 (hard)
1. Food—Juvenile poetry. 2. Children's poetry, American.
[1. Food—Poetry. 2. American poetry—Collections.]
I. Goldstein, Bobbye S.   II. Demarest, Chris L., ill.
PS595.F65W48   1992   811.008'0355—dc20   91-28794   CIP   AC

Printed in Hong Kong
Set in 13 point Sabon

The art was prepared with pen and watercolor on Arches watercolor paper.

CONTENTS

From Sleepyhead
To Breakfast Spread

Wake up, wake up
You sleepyhead!
It's time to break
The breakfast bread.

Cary Crockin

BREAKFAST TALK

"Clink clank!" say the pots and pans.
"Clatter!" says the plate.
"Sizzle!" says the bacon.
  Mom shouts, "Don't be late!"
  Clump bump, I'm down the staircase.
"Munch crunch!" says my toast.
  Mumble jumble breakfast
  Is the meal that talks the most.

Bobbi Katz

5

MUMMY SLEPT LATE AND DADDY FIXED BREAKFAST

Daddy fixed breakfast.
He made us each a waffle.
It looked like gravel pudding.
It tasted something awful.

"A little too well done? Oh well,
I'll have to start all over."
That time what landed on my plate
Looked like a manhole cover.

I tried to cut it with a fork:
The fork gave off a spark.
I tried a knife and twisted it
Into a question mark.

I tried it with a hack-saw.
I tried it with a torch.
It didn't even make a dent.
It didn't even scorch.

The next time Dad gets breakfast
When Mummy's sleeping late,
I think I'll skip the waffles.
I'd sooner eat the plate!

John Ciardi

THE TOASTER

A silver-scaled Dragon with jaws
   flaming red
Sits at my elbow and toasts my
   bread.
I hand him fat slices, and then,
   one by one,
He hands them back when he sees
   they are done.

William Jay Smith

THE MEAL

Timothy Tompkins had turnips and tea.
The turnips were tiny.
He ate at least three.
And then, for dessert,
He had onions and ice.
He liked that so much
That he ordered it twice.
He had two cups of ketchup,
A prune and a pickle.
"Delicious," said Timothy.
"Well worth a nickel."
He folded his napkin
And hastened to add,
"It's one of the loveliest breakfasts I've had."

Karla Kuskin

9

In the Mood
For a Favorite Food

A MATTER OF TASTE

What does your tongue like the most?
Chewy meat or crunchy toast?

A lumpy bumpy pickle or tickly pop?
A soft marshmallow or a hard lime drop?

Hot pancakes or a sherbet freeze?
Celery noise or quiet cheese?

Or do you like pizza
More than any of these?

Eve Merriam

The Baker
     wanted me to know
that
    underneath   the cheese
         and
sausage bits
     and
pepperoni
    slices and beneath the onions
      and mushrooms and green
          pepper
          dices

the only thing that counted
was
the
   dough

Arnold Adoff

ITALIAN NOODLES

Whenever I
Eat ravioli
I fork it quick
But chew it sloli.

A meatballed mound
Of hot spaghetti
Is what I'm rarin' for
Alretti.

Why, when it comes
To pipelike ziti—
Well, I don't know
A sight more priti.

Wouldn't you love
To have lasagna
Any old time
The mood was on ya?

Oh why oh why
Do plates of pasta
Make my heart start
Fluttering fasta?

                    X. J. Kennedy

READY FOR SPAGHETTI

Pasta ribbons, pasta bows,
Pasta spirals, pasta O's,
Some is white and some is green,
Some comes with spinach in between.

It's shaped like tubes and wheels and strings
And named all sorts of funny things:
Ravioli, tortellini,
Macaroni and linguini.

In my book it is supreme;
I like it best with peas and cream.
Pasta—there's no way to beat it.
The only thing to do is eat it!

Peggy Guthart

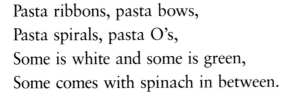

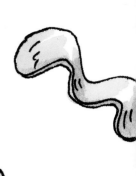

THE CODFISH

The codfish lays ten thousand eggs,
   The homely hen lays one.
The codfish never cackles
   To tell you what she's done.
And so we scorn the codfish,
   While the humble hen we prize,
Which only goes to show you
   That it pays to advertise.

Anonymous

ANIMAL CRACKERS

Animal crackers, and cocoa to drink,
That is the finest of suppers, I think;
When I'm grown up and can have what I please
I think I shall always insist upon these.
What do you choose when you're offered a treat?
When Mother says, "What would you like best to eat?"
Is it waffles and syrup, or cinnamon toast?
It's cocoa and animals that *I* love the most!

The kitchen's the coziest place that I know:
The kettle is singing, the stove is aglow,
And there in the twilight, how jolly to see
The cocoa and animals waiting for me.

Christopher Morley

15

SKINS

Skins of lemons are waterproof slickers.
Pineapple skins are stuck full of stickers.
Skins of apples are skinny and shiny
and strawberry skins (if any) are tiny.

Grapes have skins that are juicy and squishy.
Gooseberry skins are vinegar-ishy.
Skins of peaches are fuzzy and hairy.
Oranges' skins are more peely than pare-ey.

Skins of plums are squirty and squeezy.
Bananas have skins you can pull-off-easy.

I like skins that are thin as sheeting,
so what-is-under is bigger for eating.

Aileen Fisher

CELERY

Celery, raw,
Develops the jaw,
But celery, stewed,
Is more quietly chewed.

Ogden Nash

17

Time for Sweets
And Special Treats

It's such a shock, I almost screech,
When I find a worm inside my
    peach!
But then, what really makes me
    blue,
Is to find a worm who's bit in two!

William Cole

18

Into Mother's slide trombone
Liz let fall her ice cream cone.
Now when marching, Mother drips
Melting notes and chocolate chips.

X. J. Kennedy

19

FUDGE!

Oh, it poured and it rained
and it rained and it poured,
I moped round the house
feeling lonely and bored,
till Father came over
and gave me a nudge,
and said with a smile,
"Let's make chocolate fudge."

Then he gave me a bowl
that we filled to the brim,
it was fun making fudge
in the kitchen with him.
I stirred and I stirred,
but I wasn't too neat,
I got fudge on my hands,
I got fudge on my feet,
I got fudge on my shirt,
I got fudge in my hair,
I got fudge on the table
and fudge on the chair,
I got fudge in my nose,
I got fudge in my ears,
I was covered all over
with chocolate smears.

20

When the cooking was done,
Father wiped off my face,
and he frowned as he said,
"What a mess in this place!"
He was not really mad
and did not hold a grudge,
and we both ate a mountain
of chocolate fudge.

Jack Prelutsky

21

A VOTE FOR VANILLA

Vanilla, vanilla, vanilla for me,
That's the flavor I savor particularly
In cake or ice cream
Or straight from the bean
In pudding, potatoes, in fish or in stew,
In a sundae, a Monday, the whole week-long through!

Eve Merriam

MOTHER'S CHOCOLATE VALENTINE

I bought a box of chocolate hearts,
a present for my mother,
they looked so good I tasted one,
and then I tried another.

They both were so delicious
that I ate another four,
and then another couple,
and then half a dozen more.

I couldn't seem to stop myself,
I nibbled on and on,
before I knew what happened
all the chocolate hearts were gone.

I felt a little guilty,
I was stuffed down to my socks,
I ate my mother's valentine . . .
I hope she likes the box.

Jack Prelutsky

23

Eating's More Fun
Under the Stars and the Sun

STREET SONG

O, I have been walking
with a bag of potato chips,
me and potato chips
munching along,

Walking alone
eating potato chips
big old potato chips,
crunching along,

walking along
munching potato chips,
me and potato chips
lunching along.

Myra Cohn Livingston

GET 'EM HERE

"Hot dogs with sauerkraut
Cold drinks here!
Hot dogs with sauerkraut
Get 'em here!
Hot dogs with sauerkraut
Cold drinks here!"

Shouts the man as he rolls
the city's smallest store
All tucked neatly under a huge,
blue-and-orange-striped umbrella.

Lee Bennett Hopkins

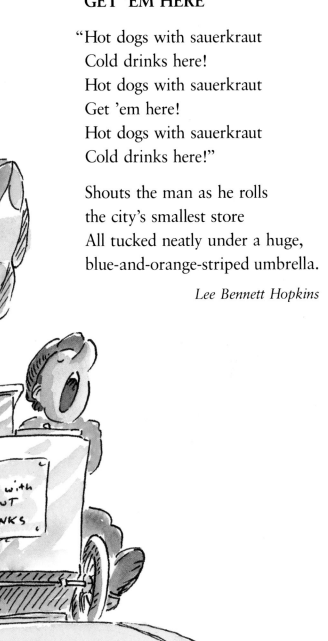

THE ICE-CREAM MAN

When summer's in the city,
   And brick's a blaze of heat,
The Ice-Cream Man with his little cart
   Goes trundling down the street.

Beneath his round umbrella,
   Oh, what a joyful sight,
To see him fill the cones with mounds
   Of cooling brown or white:

Vanilla, chocolate, strawberry,
   Or chilly things to drink
From bottles full of frosty-fizz,
   Green, orange, white, or pink.

His cart might be a flower bed
   Of roses and sweet peas,
The way the children cluster round
   As thick as honeybees.

Rachel Field

26

THE PICNIC

We brought a rug for sitting on,
Our lunch was in a box.
The sand was warm. We didn't wear
Hats or Shoes or Socks.

Waves came curling up the beach.
We waded. It was fun.
Our sandwiches were different kinds.
I dropped my jelly one.

Dorothy Aldis

28

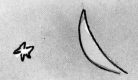

COOKOUT NIGHT

Paper cups and paper plates.
Pickles in a pickle jar.
Popcorn in a crackly bag.
Salt and pepper?
Here they are.

Paper napkins! Who forgot?
"I didn't, you did."
"I did *not*.
Besides what difference does it make?
Look at all the grass around
For wiping hands and faces on . . ."

Nothing's ever impolite:
Not outdoors on cookout night.

Dorothy Aldis

29

CHOCOLATE CAKE

I am lying in the darkness
with a smile upon my face,
as I'm thinking of my stomach,
which has got an empty space,
and that corner of the kitchen
with the piece of chocolate cake
I have got to get my hands on
for my empty stomach's sake.

When my parents both are sleeping
(I can tell by Father's snore),
I will sneak out of my bedroom,
I will tiptoe past their door,
I will slip into the kitchen
without any noise or light,
and if I'm really careful,
I will have that cake tonight.

Jack Prelutsky

GREEDY

Big pile
of

apple cores

banana skins   carrot tops

old shoes   moldy bread

toy car

dead flower   grease   meat scrap   glass jars

broken glass   burned bones

envelopes

orange peels   tin cans

headless doll   smashed board

potato peelings   soggy cardboard   coffee grounds

Here comes the garbage truck.

GOBBBBLLLLLE.

Robert Froman

31

ACKNOWLEDGMENTS

Grateful acknowledgment is made to the following for the permission to reprint copyrighted material:

Curtis Brown Ltd. for "Get 'Em Here" by Lee Bennett Hopkins from *This Street's for Me*. Text copyright © 1970 Lee Bennett Hopkins. Reprinted by permission of Curtis Brown Ltd.

William Cole for "It's such a shock I almost screech" from *Poem Stew* by William Cole, published by Lippincott. © 1967 by William Cole.

Cary Crockin for "Wake Up, Wake Up" by Cary Crockin. Granted by permission of Cary Crockin who controls all rights.

Doubleday for "The Ice Cream Man" from *A Little Book of Days* by Rachel Field. Copyright 1927 by Doubleday, a division of Bantam Doubleday Dell Publishing Group, Inc. Used by permission of Doubleday, a division of Bantam Doubleday Dell Publishing Group, Inc.

Aileen Fisher for "Skins" by Aileen Fisher from *That's Why*, Nelson, New York, 1946, copyright renewed.

Robert Froman for "Greedy" by Robert Froman from *Street Poems*. Copyright 1971 by Robert Froman.

Greenwillow Books for "Fudge" from *Rainy, Rainy, Saturday* by Jack Prelutsky. Copyright © 1980 by Jack Prelutsky. "Mother's Chocolate Valentine" from *It's Valentine's Day* by Jack Prelutsky. Copyright © 1983 by Jack Prelutsky. "Chocolate Cake" from *My Parents Think I'm Sleeping* by Jack Prelutsky. Copyright © 1985 by Jack Prelutsky. Reprinted by permission of Greenwillow Books, a division of William Morrow and Company.

Peggy Guthart for "Ready for Spaghetti" by Peggy Guthart. Copyright 1991 by Peggy Guthart.

Harper & Row, Publishers, Inc. for "Mummy Slept Late & Daddy Made Breakfast," excerpted from the poem of that name, from *You Read to Me, I'll Read to You* by John Ciardi. Copyright © 1962 by John Ciardi, published by Lippincott. "The Meal" by Karla Kuskin from *Dogs & Dragons, Trees & Dreams* by Karla Kuskin. Originally appeared in *Alexander Soames: His Poems*. Copyright © 1962 by Karla Kuskin. "Animal Crackers," excerpted from the poem of that name, from *Songs for a Little House* by Christopher Morley. Copyright 1917/45 by Christopher Morley. Reprinted by permission of Harper & Row, Publishers, Inc.

Bobbi Katz for "Breakfast Talk" by Bobbi Katz, copyright © 1978. Used by permission of the author, Bobbi Katz.

Little, Brown and Company and Curtis Brown Ltd. for "Celery" by Ogden Nash from *Verses from 1929 On* by Ogden Nash. Copyright 1941 by Ogden Nash. First appeared in *Saturday Evening Post*. Reprinted by permission of Little, Brown and Company and Curtis Brown Ltd.

Myra Cohn Livingston for "Street Song" from *The Way Things Are and Other Poems* by Myra Cohn Livingston. Copyright © 1974 by Myra Cohn Livingston. Reprinted by permission of Marian Reiner for the author.

Lothrop, Lee and Shepard Books for "The Baker" from *Eats* by Arnold Adoff. Copyright © 1979 by Arnold Adoff. Reprinted by permission of Lothrop, Lee and Shepard Books, a division of William Morrow and Company.

Margaret K. McElderry Books and Curtis Brown Ltd. for "Into Mother's Slide Trombone" by X.J. Kennedy. Reprinted with permission of Margaret K. McElderry Books, an imprint of Macmillan Publishing Company, and Curtis Brown Ltd. from *Brats* by X.J. Kennedy. Copyright © 1986 by X.J. Kennedy. "Italian Noodles" by X.J. Kennedy. Reprinted with permission of Margaret K. McElderry Books, an imprint of Macmillan Publishing Company, and Curtis Brown Ltd. from *Ghastlies, Goops and Pincushions* by X.J. Kennedy. Copyright © 1989 by X.J. Kennedy.

Eve Merriam for "A Matter of Taste" and "A Vote for Vanilla," excerpted from the poem of that name, from *Jamboree: Rhymes for All Times* by Eve Merriam. Copyright © 1962, 1964, 1966, 1973, 1984 by Eve Merriam. Reprinted by permission of Marian Reiner for the author.

G.P. Putnam's Sons for "Cookout Night" by Dorothy Aldis from *Is Anybody Hungry?* by Dorothy Aldis. Copyright © 1964 by Dorothy Aldis. "The Picnic" by Dorothy Aldis from *Hop, Skip, and Jump!* by Dorothy Aldis, copyright 1934, copyright © renewed 1961 by Dorothy Aldis. Reprinted by permission of G.P. Putnam's Sons.

William Jay Smith for "The Toaster" by William Jay Smith from *Laughing Time: Nonsense Poems*, published by Delacorte Press, 1980. Copyright © by William Jay Smith 1955, 1957, 1980. Reprinted by permission of William Jay Smith.